Baby Talk

To Mum, Dad and Gavin
S.S.

BABY TALK
A PICTURE CORGI BOOK 0 552 52647 9

First published in Great Britain by Doubleday,
a division of Transworld Publishers Ltd

PRINTING HISTORY
Doubleday edition published 1990
Picture Corgi edition published 1992
Reprinted 1992,1993,1994 (twice),1995 (twice)

Picture Corgi Books are published by Transworld Publishers Ltd., 61-63 Uxbridge Road, Ealing, London W5 5SA, in Australia by Transworld Publishers (Australia) Pty. Ltd., 15-25 Helles Avenue, Moorebank, NSW 2170, and in New Zealand by Transworld Publishers (N.Z.) Ltd., 3 William Pickering Drive, Albany, Auckland.

Made and printed in Portugal by Printer Portuguesa

Baby Talk

Annie David *illustrated by Sami Sweeten*

PICTURE CORGI BOOKS

Contents

Dirty and smelly

Thrills

Animal talk

Engines and wheels

Sharing and helping

Crying

Cosy cuddles

Kissing

Saying goodbye

Time for bed

Hello!

Boo!

Look!

Hee! Hee!

More!

Mmmmm!

All gone!

Mummy!

Daddy!

No!

Hot!

Oh dear!

Pooh!

Dirty!

Oooh!

Miaow
Woof

Moo
Baa
Quack

Brrrm! Brrrm!

Mine!

Waaah!

Cuddle!

Kiss!

Bye, bye

Night, night